# ORLANDO
## (The Marmalade Cat)

# A SEASIDE HOLIDAY
## By Kathleen Hale

Frederick Warne

FREDERICK WARNE

Published by the Penguin Group
27 Wrights Lane, London W8 5TZ, England
Penguin Books USA Inc., 375 Hudson Street, New York, New York 10014, USA
Penguin Books Australia Ltd, Ringwood, Victoria, Australia
Penguin Books Canada Ltd, 2801 John Street, Markham, Ontario, Canada L3R 1B4
Penguin Books (NZ) Ltd, 182-190 Wairau Road, Auckland 10, New Zealand

Penguin Books Ltd, Registered Offices: Harmondsworth, Middlesex, England

First published 1952 by Country Life Ltd
This revised edition first published 1991 by Frederick Warne & Co.

10 9 8 7 6 5 4

ISBN 0 7232 3651 8

Printed in Singapore by Imago Publishing Limited

The illustrations in this book were originally drawn direct by the author on 'Plastocowell', a transparent plastic material used in lithography and lithographed by W.S. Cowell Ltd. For this edition the type has been reset and the illustrations scanned from a first edition.

O RLANDO wanted to take his dear wife Grace and their three kittens – the tortoiseshell Pansy, the snow-white Blanche and little black Tinkle – to the sea for their summer holiday; but all the hotels and boarding-houses were full and there was not even room for an extra canary, let alone a whole family of cats.

Orlando was very unhappy, for the hot weather had made Grace pale and tired and the kittens had quite lost their appetites; they would not even eat the shrimps that Grace had bought them for a treat.

"They're like fried spectacles," grumbled Tinkle, "so prickly."

The cats lay panting on the stairs opposite the open front door. They were too hot to go up or down.

Suddenly there was a piercing whistle which ended in a deep shuddery noise – it was Vulcan the horse neighing on the door-step, and he clumped along the hall to the cats.

"Me and the Missis and the little 'un be on our way to Owlbarrow-on-Sea," he said, and snorted loudly as horses do. "We'd be mighty glad if you'd come along of us; the waggon's at the gate and there be acres of room for you all." Vulcan stamped (for there was a tickle in his hoof), which shook the hat-stand and rattled the umbrellas.

"But," said Orlando gloomily, "there'll be no room for us when we get there. Everywhere's full up."

"Nay! Nay!" said Vulcan merrily. "There be space for ninety cats and more where we do be a-goin'! We've got an old ship, ye see; it be moored on land, high and dry on the banks of the River Owl, just where it do run into the sea."

"A ship!" squealed the kittens. "How *frilling*!"

"We shall be delighted to accept your kind invitation," purred Orlando gratefully, and the kittens bounced up and down on the mat like hot pop-corn. Grace collected everything they would need by the sea, while Orlando fetched the trunk.

"Don't forget to pack my pet spider!" squeaked Tinkle in between bounces.

"I've not forgotten," mewed Grace from inside the trunk.

Orlando went round the house to make sure no taps were dripping and no lights were left on; then he put a note out with the milk bottles to tell the milkman the family were going on holiday.

The cats were soon ready, and Vulcan gently lifted them up by the scruffs of their necks into the waggon, beside his dear wife Venus and their little brown foal.

Vulcan backed in between the shafts of the waggon. After Orlando had fastened the buckles of the harness, Vulcan took the reins in his mouth and drove himself and his passengers towards Owlbarrow-on-Sea.

As Vulcan pulled the waggon along the streets everybody noticed the little foal and said loudly, "Oh the *darling*! How *sweet* he is!" Tinkle did not like this at all, for he was used to being everybody's pet himself.

"What's your name?" Tinkle asked the little foal severely.

"Cupid," he shyly answered.

"Have you ever been to the sea before?" asked Tinkle.

"No," smiled Cupid.

"Pooh!" said Tinkle scornfully, "*I* have!"

"Oh you *fibber*!" cried Pansy and Blanche.

Tinkle was suddenly ashamed of himself and he muttered, "Of *course* I've been to see – lots 'n lots of fings, wiv my own eyes."

"Oh Tinkle, you *are* a clever joker," laughed Cupid admiringly, and Tinkle began to like the little foal, he was so kind and friendly.

"I'll show you marbellous fings when we get to the sea," Tinkle boasted. "Sea-horses, sea-lions, sea-cows, sea-efflunts, cat-fish, dog-fish, pore-pussies, crobs, labsters, shrumps 'n jellie-bags 'n – 'n . . . ."

"Tinkle, how *wonderful* you are. You know everything!" gasped Cupid.

*Clip clop, clip clop,* went Vulcan's hooves on the road; he swished his long tail from side to side to keep away the flies, and snorted the dust out of his nostrils; Venus snorted in reply so that he would not feel lonely. The cats purred with happiness and sometimes their teeth chattered with excitement. They travelled all day and Venus changed places with Vulcan from time to time, to give him a rest.

Vulcan climbed the last hill by the light of a beautiful orange sunset. There lay Owlbarrow on the slope below them; it glowed like a fairy city in the heart of a coal fire, beside the flame-coloured sea.

It was magical! The animals held their breath for fear the tiniest puff of air might blow it all away.

"It be real enough," grinned Vulcan, and the waggon pushed him gently downhill, as though it wanted to see for itself.

The weary travellers jogged down to where the River Owl ran into the sea, just outside the little town, and there was the old ship, propped up on the bank, and tarred black all over. A huge door in the side, near the ground, opened into a stable for the horses, which was also the dining-room for all the animals; a ladder up the side led to the cabins and deck for the cats.

A flock of hens marched backwards out of the great door, scratching away the dust behind them until the floor inside was perfectly clean; pigeons fluttered in and out of the port-holes and, like feather dusters, they brushed off all the cobwebs.

A large bundle of straw on two legs walked towards the travellers and cried, "Welcome to Howlbarrow!" Then the bundle was thrown on to the ground by the plump, smiling old woman who had been carrying it on her head. She wore gum-boots, breeches, a jersey, lots of brooches and necklaces, and numbers of fancy hair-slides in the shapes of animals, flowers and True Lovers' Knots decorated her grey hair.

"I'm a land-girl," she explained. "Me name's Salubrious 'cos I'm allus 'appy – Sally for short. You'll quite fall in love with me – everybody allus does."

Indeed the whole party liked her at once, she was so kind and twinkly.

While Vulcan unloaded the waggon, Sally led the cats up the ladder and showed them their cabins. There were bunks to sleep in, one above the other, and a wonderful view of the sea. A dear little shiny black sofa, with brown feet and cushions, provided specially for Grace, stood in her cabin. The cats unpacked and arranged their belongings while Tinkle fed his spider with a fly-pie he had made.

Down below in the horses' stable was a big bed for Vulcan, Venus and Cupid. Above Venus's straw pillow was a manger filled with hay, in case she felt hungry in the night; Vulcan had one with books in it and a reading lamp; in Cupid's was a doll with legs of parsnips and a turnip head. There was a charming dressing-table for Venus, draped with curtains of straw looped back with rope and pretty bunches of carrots; the mirror was a water trough of clean water.

Venus unpacked her scarlet tasselled ear-nets, the nose-bags, Vulcan's sun-bonnet, blinkers, spare shoes and a clean collar, then she looked at herself in her mirror, tidied her fringe and smiled under her curly moustache.

"I'm just a-goin' now," called Sally, "to get your supper – see you later – if all goes well," and off she waddled followed by her hens and pigeons.

While Sally prepared the supper, the cats rode the horses down to the sea by the light of the moon.

The only person on the shore was an old man called Mr. Curmudgeon, who hated everyone so much that he only came out when everybody else had gone in. He scowled at Vulcan and Venus as they cantered past through the frothy surf, cooling their tired hooves, but they did not notice him.

The cats clung to the horses and enjoyed the glorious ride by the moonlit sea.

"It's like a 'normous fish with silver scales," whispered Pansy.

"And it sort of purrs," mewed Blanche. Tinkle was quite silent for the first time in his little life.

"Hi, Tinkle!" whinnied Cupid. "Where are all the animals you promised to show me?"

"Gone to bed," muttered Tinkle. "Mermaids are tucking them up at the bottom of the sea."

The ship looked very snug when the animals returned, with a stable lantern shining down on the supper table. There were clover-and-hay sandwiches for the horses, and each cat had a saucer of milk nicely flavoured by a floating sprat, and a dish of what Tinkle called "Fish-in-Ships". Sally had put a vase of flowers on the table and barrels for the animals to sit on.

Cupid was so hungry that he ate the flowers as well as his supper, and the kittens had three helpings of everything until they bulged like little footballs.

Orlando and Grace were pleased, for they had been so worried over the kittens' lost appetites.

"It only remains, dear Grace," said Orlando, "for you to get those roses back in your cheeks, and everything will be perfect."

"Dog-roses, I suppose you mean!" laughed Grace gaily; "but," she added seriously, "there's one thing needed to make *me* happy, it's to see those wrinkles on your forehead go away. You've worried about us so much that you've frowned your stripes all together." She gently licked Orlando's brow and smoothed out the wrinkles.

"*That's* better," she softly purred.

After supper Sally cleared the table and the animals decided to go to bed.

"Good-night All," said Sally. "See you in the mornin' – if all goes well."

The cats were so sleepy that they had each to hold on to the other's tail as they climbed the ladder to their cabins. Moonbeams shone through the port-holes and Tinkle could see the eyes of his pet spider gleaming on his pillow.

Grace sat on the sofa to undress and then sprang into bed.

Suddenly the sofa shook itself, opened a pink mouth and yawned, turned round and round and then lay down on its cushions! The 'sofa' was not a sofa at all, but a nice fat dachshund called Daisy.

The next morning Sally brought the animals' breakfasts, and a picnic lunch and tea for them to take on to the beach. "I'm just a-comin'!" she called. "Wake hup! Sun's shinin' and sea's as warm as soup," and she laughed to see the horses' huge pink mouths yawning, and the cats' neat little pink ones gaping like pinched snapdragon flowers.

"*Ooo!*" cried Tinkle, when he saw his delicious breakfast. "Scrambled Legs!"

When Daisy had eaten some biscuits she made herself into a sofa again, for Grace to sit on while she dressed.

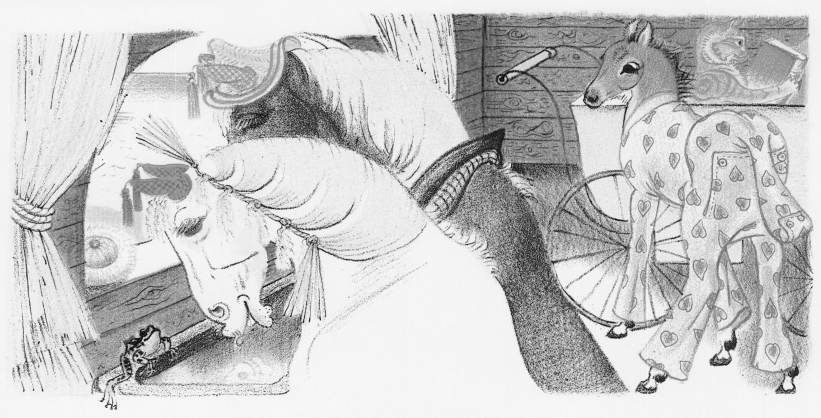

After breakfast Venus put on her ear-nets to keep away the flies, and Vulcan his sun-bonnet and the clean collar; Orlando packed everything the animals would need into Cupid's pram, to which he harnessed the little foal, who loved pulling it. Tinkle climbed on top and they led the way to the sea; Daisy kept close to Grace.

Brightly painted boats lay on the beach, coloured towels and bathing costumes were spread out to dry, and their owners lay in the sunshine eating ices. The little town behind, with its houses perched one above the other up the hill, was gay with flags; salmon-pink and cod-white flowers grew in the window boxes and gardens; people bobbed in and out of their windows on to balconies, like the cuckoos of cuckoo-clocks. Orlando fetched a

deck-chair for himself and Grace. Vulcan scooped out comfortable hollows in the sand for himself and Venus; he opened a book and put on his blinkers to read, for they kept his eyes from straying from the page. The kittens ran down to the sea to play with the waves. Cupid trotted off to nibble the flowers on a lady's straw hat nearby, and she so loved Cupid that she gave him the rest of the hat to eat.

Grace decided to bathe and she crept under an upturned boat to change into her costume.

"I don't like the idea," said Orlando nervously.

"I shall be quite safe, dear," mewed Grace from under the boat, her eyes shining like green lamps in the darkness. "My costume is waterproof and will fill up with air, in the sea, so that I shall float on the top of the water."

Soon Grace appeared in her navy blue costume with a sailor's-collar, bloomers down to her ankles, and a special long bag for her tail, with an anchor embroidered on the tip; she danced gaily down to the sea and her tail waved to and fro inside its bag. She waded through the surf; her costume filled with air and billowed around her; Daisy followed her closely and Orlando waited anxiously on the beach. Soon Grace began to float happily upon the glass-green sea.

Suddenly a wave burst into tumbling foam, rushed down the collar of Grace's costume and pushed all the air along to the tip of her tail-piece; the tail-piece floated, but poor Grace hung downwards in the water. But before she had time to be frightened, Daisy dived after her, grabbed the sailor-collar in her teeth, and pulled her the right way up and back to the shore.

Orlando was trembling with fright as he helped his dear wife up the beach, dripping wet and trailing her balloon-like tail behind her.

"Oh dear," sighed Grace. "I was enjoying myself so much...never mind, let's have lunch," and she crept under the boat to change her costume.

One morning, after several calm, sunny days, Tinkle awoke to see fluffy white clouds like Persian kittens scudding across the sky, blown by a wind that whistled round the old ship.

"Glory! Glory! Glory!" he squealed. "At last I can fly my kite!"

Very soon the animals were on the beach and Orlando spread out the beautiful kite, with its long tail with tufts of pretty coloured paper.

Suddenly a gust of wind blew the kite up into the air; the kittens grabbed the string that held it, and Orlando and Grace seized the kittens, but the wind whirled the kite and the cats high above the people on the beach. Grace's big hat acted like a sail and so did Pansy's and Blanche's gym tunics.

Cupid saw the tufted tail whisk past and, thinking it would be nice to eat, he cantered after it. Vulcan and Venus galloped after Cupid.

The kite flew so close to the houses that Orlando was able to knock on one of the windows for help but, alas, it belonged to old Mr. Curmudgeon, who angrily shut it.

It was pleasant, however, sailing through the air, and the cats began to enjoy themselves. When the town had been left far behind, the wind fell and the kite lowered them gently on to some rocks beside a deep pool. Cupid came galloping along, followed by his parents.

Slippery seaweed fringed the edge of the pool and the water was cloudy with sand.

"Keep still," whispered Orlando. "We frightened lots of sea creatures, who churned up the sand when they dashed away to hide; it will settle and we shall see wonderful things in the pool."

The water began to clear, red and green blobs of jelly which stuck to the rocks opened out like flowers, a little crab ran sideways across the floor of the pool, and a speckled fish with whiskers darted from under a stone. Suddenly Tinkle arched his back and fluffed up his tail. "I see a mermaid!" he screeched.

There on the sandy bottom of the pool lay a mysterious shape; it was as long as a crocodile, with a pinkish face, silky green hair, black eyes and a long thick tail like an eel, with a frilly end.

"Who will volunteer," shouted the Lord Mayor, "for the dangerous job of being captain?"

Orlando sprang forward and saluted: he opened his mouth to say "I will," but the howling tempest snatched his voice away.

The Lord Mayor hugged him gratefully, but Orlando struggled to free himself, for there was no time to be lost. As he leapt on board the life-boat, it swiftly glided down the slip-way into the sea with a mighty *Whoooosh!*

"They're off!" yelled the crowd, though not a word could be heard above the gale.

Grace and the kittens clung to the horses' hairy ankles to avoid being blown away; everybody anxiously watched the life-boat tossing on the tops of enormous waves and then sinking out of sight behind them. There were terrible moments when it seemed as though the boat was lost, but at last it reached the wreck.

All the watchers on the beach had but one thought – "Can Orlando bring them back to safety?" But the brave crew did exactly as Orlando bade them and he steered the life-boat, with the rescued people on board, through the heaving sea back to the shore.

It seemed to Grace as though a whole week had passed since her dear husband had left her side, a week of terrible anxiety.

Poor Orlando was wet to the skin and shivering; Grace tried to lick him dry and Vulcan wanted to take him home in Cupid's pram, which the faithful Daisy had been guarding.

"B-but, first," Orlando stammered through his chattering teeth, "I m-must see that these shipwrecked p-people are g-given hot meals, b-baths and b-beds."

The people from the shipwreck were stiff with cold. The kind folk of Owlbarrow took the strangers to their homes and made them comfortable, except one, for whom there was no room. This was Queen Catalpa, who had waited until all her people had been cared for. Suddenly Orlando thought of Mr. Curmudgeon sitting alone in his house.

"Grace, my love," he whispered, "ask Mr. Curmudgeon to look after Queen Catalpa – if anyone can soften his heart, you can."

Grace knocked on Mr. Curmudgeon's front door: it opened two inches and the old man's long yellow face peered out.

"Please, dear Mr. Curmudgeon," pleaded Grace, "can you give Queen Catalpa a hot bath, a warm bed and something to eat?"

"Certainly not!" he snapped, and almost shut the door – but not quite, for nobody had ever called him "dear" before, and he longed to hear Grace say it again.

"Dear, *dear* Mr. Curmudgeon," purred Grace winningly.

"Oh, all right," the old man muttered. "Bring her in."

The house was dirty and untidy, which shocked the Queen.

Orlando dried himself by the fire, while Queen Catalpa lay in a hot bath. Grace followed Mr. Curmudgeon into the kitchen to see if she could help him, and found him mixing a horrid mess of raw onions, peppermint creams and fish for supper.

"Dear Mr. Curmudgeon," she said, "you have far too much to do. Let *me* do the cooking." He was delighted, for there was nothing he hated more.

Grace scrambled eggs and boiled some milk. The kittens took the Queen her supper in bed.

"Mother cooked this," they told her. "Mr. Curmudgeon doesn't know how to!"

"The poor lamb," smiled the Queen. "I'll cook for him while I'm here."

Mr. Curmudgeon and the cats sat round the fire and ate their "scrambled legs"; the old man enjoyed his especially, and told Grace that his own cooking always gave him tummy-aches and sleepless nights, which made him so cross that nobody liked him.

The next morning the cats called on the Queen, and were glad to find her well and happy; Mr. Curmudgeon was already less yellow and more cheerful, for he had slept soundly after Grace's nice supper.

Grace showed the Queen how to use Mr. Curmudgeon's vacuum-cleaner, which was as bad-tempered as its owner. In a few days the house was clean and Mr. Curmudgeon had never been so well; he dearly loved his "Catty," as he called the Queen.

Queen Catalpa asked Orlando to have a new ship made for her, and off he went to Mr. Rope the ship-builder, who promised to begin at once.

One day the new ship was finished; Mr. Rope had carved one end to look like Orlando's head and the other like his tail; it was painted orange and striped like marmalade, with pale blue sails to match Grace's apron. It was very beautiful.

The people of Owlbarrow and their friends were sad at parting, for they loved each other. Suddenly Queen Catalpa began to cry.

"Darling Mudgy," she sobbed down Mr. Curmudgeon's neck, "I can't bear to leave you. I'll live here and marry you."

"Oh Catty dear," he murmured, "how *lovely!*"

"But what shall we do without a queen?" cried the people anxiously.

"Wait a moment," said Orlando, and disappeared. He returned with Sally, who galloped along the shore carrying a suit-case full of hair-slides and brooches and followed by her hens and pigeons.

"I'm just a-comin'!" she panted. "I'll be queen – if all goes well."

The people were very pleased, for a land-girl would be able to help them grow their corn and look after their pigs.

"See you later!" cried Queen Sally as she sailed away with her poultry and her people to the other side of the world.

"And now we, too, must be going," said Vulcan to Orlando, "for our holiday be over."

The End